NOW I KNOW

EILEEN DISTASIO-CLARK

With Great Love and Appreciation to those who Have and Do Bless My Life

My Family:

Joseph DeStasio Sr. & Miriam Lucille Baragone DeStasio, My Late Parents.

Andrea Jean DeStasio McIntosh, My Older Sister and their Family.

Joseph DeStasio Jr., My Younger and Only Brother and their Family.

Donna Marie DeStasio Wagner, My Younger Sister and their Family.

My Children:

Eileen, Rebekah, Rachel, S. Michael,

Jennifer, Sharon, Tara, Stephanie,

Apryll, Mikaelah, & M. Trevor

and THEIR Families!!

ACKNOWLEDGMENTS

First and foremost, I express, deeply, my sincere gratitude to our Heavenly Father for blessing me with the gift and talent of writing! I know I could not do what I do without His assistance.

I also want to acknowledge and express gratitude to the members of my birth family—Joseph Sr., Miriam, Andrea, Joseph Junior, and Donna. All the experiences of my childhood years, experiences that taught me so very much and enabled me to reveal my true self to myself, came about through my experiences and relationships with them.

And, of course, it goes without saying, but I will say it anyway: I also want to acknowledge and note my gratitude to my children, Eileen, Rebekah, Rachel, S. Michael, Jennifer, Sharon, Tara, Stephanie, Apryll, Mikaelah, and M. Trevor, and their families! Through multiple things they said to me, over multiple years, I finally came to the realization that Heavenly Father gave me the gift of writing and opened the doors to these experiences because He knew that by sharing them with others, others could feel His love too.

And He definitely wants us all to know that He, Heavenly Father, Heavenly Mother, and Jehovah truly do loves us!!!

INTRODUCTION

There are sixteen books in this series, which I refer to as *"The Ellie Series."* All of the characters in these stories portray real people from my life. The main characters depict the members of my family: Daddy is my daddy; Mommy is my mommy; Jeannie is my older sister; Junior is my brother; Maria is my younger sister; and Ellie is me. Now, those are not our actual first names, but they do reference us.

The first story in the series presents our Heavenly Father's Plan of Salvation and takes place in the Pre-Earth World. Now, of course, because we all—when we were born—received what is known as The Veil of Forgetfulness, I do not actually remember everything from or about the Pre-Earth World, but I do know about and understand it from much study and worship as a member of The Church of Jesus Christ of Latter-Day Saints, and memories restored to me through the Holy Spirit. So, from this story there is much truth to be learned.

The last story in the series is set in the Post-Mortal World, and presents a depiction of what happens to us after this life. Again, because I have not gone there yet, I cannot say I 'remember' this. But, I have also learned about the Post-Mortal World from much study and worship as a member of The Church of Jesus Christ of Latter-Day Saints.

All of the other stories are based on true events from my life; events that actually occurred when and how they are depicted in these stories. I chose these events because they are among the many occurrences in my life that presented, or revealed that which I already knew without having to be taught, Principles of Eternal Truths.

Also, I chose these events as the settings for my stories because they depict wonderful learning moments from my childhood and adolescent years, lessons that have blessed and benefited me throughout the whole of my life and will forever continue to do so. Also, through these great truths and their consequences in my life, I have been able to share them with many others, whose lives have also been blessed by them.

So, please read and enjoy, then care and share the messages and stories with others!!

Now, there are also a couple of things you can look for:

In each story, the title of the previous story is presented in *italicized* form, the title of the next story is presented in *Capitalized Italicized* form, and the title of the story being read is presented in **emboldened** form.

Also, every story has at least one word that is uncommon or 'created.'

So, as you read, search, find, and have fun!

NOW I KNOW

It had been the most awesomely amazing experience Ellie had ever had! I say that because she was awed; she was amazed; she was speechless!! But more than anything thing else, she was grateful!!! As she walked along the path from the front of the Provo Temple to the back of the Provo Temple, then down that same path to the temple grounds entrance, through the gate onto Temple Hill Drive, which took her to Temple View Drive, then back to 900 East, which was where Heritage Halls, her dorm was. She thought, and thought, and thou… okay, so I am sure you know what she did. She thought about what she had experienced and the great good it had done, was doing, and always would be doing for her! In fact, she thought about how it had put so many things into perspective!

For one, she thought about her last year in high school, when she had applied to and been accepted by fifteen different colleges in the United States and Europe, but she had not chosen to go to any of them. She did not really know why. It had not made any sense to her because she knew that she really did want to go to college. But, at least then, it just did not feel right. Of course, she did learn later that…

Hey! Wait! Let us 'step into her thoughts!' That way you can have a better understanding of what she had understood about why none of those colleges had felt right. Are you okay with that? You are! Great!! Then let us be stepping!!

It was a comfortably warm, nicely sunshiny early Friday evening in June; Ellie, with her Daddy and Mommy, had gone to the Callister's house to talk to the missionaries about the gospel.

Oh! Wait a minute! Maybe I should explain something to you so that what you learn about 'that moment' makes more sense. Should I do that? Hmmm, yes, I think I should. So, I will.

Perhaps you remember, but just in case you do not, I will remind you that when Ellie was just seventeen years old and graduating from high school, she thought she wanted to be a nun, because she thought that was what God would want her to do, because that is what she had been taught in her Catechism classes. But she also knew that she really did not want to be separated from her family. So, when her Daddy had asked her to wait until she was eighteen to make that decision, she was completely happy to comply. However, because she really did think that that was what God would want her to do, and she always wanted to do what God wanted her to do. She decided to spend that time—the three months between graduation and her eighteenth birthday—reading the

Bible and studying the history of the Catholic Church, in preparation for the Convent. And that was what she had done, but not to the conclusion that she had expected.

When Ellie had finished reading the Bible, which was just before her birthday, she was not ready to go to the Convent and knew that she never would be, because, from all that she had read and learned, she was absolutely convinced that either the Catholic Church was true and the Bible was not, or the Bible was true and the Catholic Church was not, but they could not both be true because they were not saying the same things!

Now, that made Ellie rather sad; not because she was no longer going to become a nun, but because she realized that she did not have God's truth. And that was what she wanted more than she wanted anything else. But Ellie was not one to ever give up when she knew that what she wanted or was doing was worth having or accomplishing. So, that was when and why she decided to look for the truth. In fact, she asked God to help her. She told Him, if there really was truth in this world, and He would lead her to it, she would live it, no matter what that meant. And so began the journey that did lead her to the truth.

She wondered, at first, how she would go about searching for the truth. It was not something tangible, like gold or stone or books or... well, you get the idea.

It was intangible, but it was also the most important thing for us to have. So, after quite a bit of thought and prayers, she decided the best place to start was to learn what other religions taught.

Now, she did not really believe any other church could be God's church because, as she reasoned, since the Catholic Church, which had originally been established by Jesus, no longer taught all truth because of political and ecclesiastical corruption, then no other church could be true either, because they all had either broken away from one church or another, or they were established by a man, and man could NOT form God's church. She was certain, without the slightest inkling of a doubt, that there could only be a true church, if God Himself, would come back to establish it. And she knew that, if He did that, He would have called prophets again, and apostles, and evangelists, and... well, you know what I mean. He would have to have established for us now, what He had established for them then, but He had not done that... or so she thought.

Anyway, not really knowing why that seemed like the right way to begin, that was still the way she began. And that was how she learned about the Latter-Day Saints, and was, after almost two years of religious study, interaction with the Latter-Day Saints that she had met, and miraculous experiences that could only have come from God when she was nineteen years old, well, a little more than nineteen and a half years old. She had been baptized into The Church of Jesus Christ of Latter-Day Saints. But she was only baptized because she knew, with unwavering, absolute certainty, that that was what Heavenly Father wanted her to do. She could not really say that she actually had her own testimony of its truth. She wondered if Heavenly Father was testing her so that she could see if she really would do what He said even when she did not understand the reason why. Now, of course, even that would not deter her from doing what she knew God wanted her to do, so she did!

Now, without going into too much detail, I know I have a tendency to make short stories long, and long stories longer, and longer, and lo... uh, I am pretty certain you already know what I am saying so, I will just stop there and continue with what I was saying.

When Ellie got baptized, even though she had gotten permission from her parents to do so, her daddy was not happy about that, but for some reason, he agreed to listen to the discussions taught by the missionaries at the Callister's home, and it was a good discussion.

Okay, so now we can go back to Ellie's thoughts.

As the Stations: Daddy, Mommy, and Ellie, left the Callister's house and were headed out to their car,

Ellie had an amazing **now I know** realization. It was at that moment that she finally understood why she had not chosen any of those fifteen colleges to attend. It was not that college was wrong for her. It was that she had not applied to the college that was right for her, Brigham Young University. Truth be told when she was submitting applications, she had not yet even heard of BYU.

So, Ellie thought, Heavenly Father was helping me make the right choice, and I did not even know that. *If I had gone to college, any other college when I got out of high school, I would have missed the opportunity to go to the right college. Yes, I would have been younger when I began college, just eighteen years old, instead of the twenty years old that I am now, but my life would have been so much different than it is now, and that probably would not have been good in any way! Wow! I am so grateful! But now, now that I am here, I am so homesick. But I will not go home, no, at least not yet! Not until Heavenly Father tells me the time is right. Besides, I really do want to complete my degree.*

As Ellie approached Shipp Hall, the Heritage Halls dorm in which she was residing, she looked up at the mountain and thought about one of the scriptures that spoke of the establishment of Heavenly Father's true church. Even though she had never taken the time to memorize it, the words came into her mind and solidified the experience she had just had at the temple grounds.

*****Uh, Side Note:** This is that scripture: Isaiah 2: 2, "And it shall come to pass in the last days, that the mountain of the Lord's house shall be established in the top of the mountains, and shall be exalted above the hills; and all nations shall flow unto it."

Now, back to the other side.***

Rather than going into the dorm, Ellie decided to go to the Wilkinson Student Center, where she could sit in the warmth of one of the lounges that faced the mountain and, as she looked at the mountain, ponder what she had just experienced. She was quite happy to see, when she got there, that the lounge of her choice was just about empty. That was definitely her preference and because of that, she was able to choose a seat close to the window.

As she looked up over the mountain, she thought about the words of that scripture. She realized how perfectly that identified The Church of Jesus Christ of Latter-Day Saints. Its headquarters was in Salt Lake City—in the mountains. But its members were all around the world—in other nations! What could be more evidential of its truthfulness, its authenticity, its correctness?

"Nothing," Ellie whispered, "nothing! And I know that because He told me, showed me, in a way that nothing will ever nor could ever challenge!" Her thoughts then went back to the temple grounds and she mentally relived that experience.

Okay! I think we should just 'step back into her thoughts' again. Ready? You are! Of course, you are, because you really want to know what happened. So, here we go!

As Ellie walked back to her dorm after her last class ended, she was thinking, *This is not working! I felt so good about coming to BYU, and I do want to complete college, but I am so homesick! I feel alone and lonely, out of place, like a stranger. I miss my family and I really want to be with them—to be home—but I know this is where I should be.*

Once in her room, as Ellie put her books down on her desk and laid down on her bed, she began to realize that little by little, day after day, the need had been increasing for her to know, really know, not just hope or believe, but KNOW that The Church of Jesus Christ of Latter-Day Saints really was God's one true church. She needed to know for herself, not just because others were telling her, that the gospel taught by the Latter-Day Saints really was God's gospel, all the truth that He had thus far revealed. She realized that, while her interactions within the church had been wonderful and most desirable, she had not really gained a testimony of their validity. Now, because she was feeling so miserable being away from her family, she knew, in a way that she had not realized before, that she absolutely needed to truly know that the choice she had made, in joining the church, was the right thing to do because it is the right church. That was why she made the decision to go to the temple grounds the next day, which was Friday, the 25th of January, 1974, and talk to Heavenly Father, which is exactly what she had done.

It was a cold day; it was snowing and somewhat gloomy. Nevertheless, she did, as she told herself she would do, go up to the Provo Temple, walked to the front of the temple. She was happy to see that there was no one there. Ellie knelt-down on the cold, hard, stone-paved path, and began praying.

She told Heavenly Father everything she was thinking, feeling, wanting, and needing. She told Him about everything she had ever done wrong, from smacking her sister when she was a tiny tot, to being proud of herself when she got *the ticket* for driving 105 miles-per-hour in a fifty-five-mile-per-hour zone, to breaking a window because she was angry, to scolding one of her high school teachers for being unkind to one of her classmates, to... and... well, you get the idea, everything she could think of.

She begged for forgiveness for all those wrongs and all the ones she could not remember. She expressed gratitude for every blessing she could recognize and recall, as well as for all the ones she could not. And then she begged Him to tell her if she had done the right thing, to let her know if this was His church, if this gospel was His truth. She prayed, and prayed, and prayed, and... well, again, I know you get the idea. Yet, there was nothing, no answer, no whisper, no feeling.

By the time she finished her prayer, she was beyond freezing, wet from the snow, and had dents in her knees from the stone pavement. Her muscles ached and she needed to go back to the dorm to thaw out. As she stood up, looking upward, she told Heavenly Father, "I have to go warm up, but I WILL be back. I... need... to... know!"

Then, just as she began to turn to leave, there appeared a glow, like sunshine, on the front temple wall. The words, House of the Lord—Holiness to the Lord—The Church of Jesus Christ of Latter-Day Saints, shimmered and shined in a way that she had never seen anything shine! She looked behind her at the mountaintop, expecting to see the sun shining, but all she saw were clouds and snow. Yet, when she looked back at the temple wall, there it was—that glow. After a few moments, as she gazed intently, trying to understand what she was seeing, the words, The Church of Jesus Christ of Latter-Day Saints, seemed to lift off the wall and, appearing as little torches, float towards her.

So real did they seem that, when they were just in front of her and a little above her head, she actually reached up to touch them. But as she did, one by one, they fell, and as each one fell, a feeling of warmth, that burning feeling of the spirit, grew inside of her. When the last torch fell, she knew with a full heart, tears of joy, an overarching peace, and crystal clarity of mind, with absolute surety, unquestionable certainty, undeniable conviction, and unconquerable power that

The Church of Jesus Christ of Latter-Day Saints **IS** indeed the **ONE TRUE** church of our **ONE** and **ONLY** God, and that the gospel it teaches is, the **INFINITE**, **UNDENIABLE**, **LIVING** word of **THAT** God!

As Ellie left the Wilkinson Student Center, she realized, with indescribable assurance and absolute spiritual confirmation, that she could never and would never be able to deny the testimony of the truthfulness of both the church and its gospel that she had received. She also knew that her testimony was, indeed, a marvelous, precious, timeless, priceless gift from Heavenly Father. She was completely sure that if ever there came a time when she fell into inactivity or left the church, it could only be because of pride, arrogance, self-aggrandizement, or outright rebellion. But it could never be because she did not know that it was true!! Because she did now know that it IS true! She did not just believe it; she knew it! She knew that she knew it!! She knew that she always would know it!!! And she knew that she could never not know it!!!!

She could say to herself, and she did; **now I know** why so many people, even other churches, persecute and lie about The Church of Jesus Christ of Latter-Day Saints. What church would Satan want to destroy? None other than God's church! No other could get people back to where we all said we wanted to be, to where Satan could never return, back to our Heavenly Home!!

So grateful was Ellie for the marvelous testimony that she had been given that when she got back to her dorm, she pulled out her cassette recorder. Yes, you read it correctly, cassette recorder and a blank tape, and recorded her experience. She determined that, on Monday, she would go to the campus post office, package it up, and send it home to her family. She was hoping that her testimony and the experience of how she gained it, would assist her family in gaining their testimonies.

Side Note:** Her younger sister, Maria, had already listened to the missionary lessons, gained her testimony, and been baptized before Ellie had even left for school. But Daddy and Mommy, Jeannie, and Junior had not, not yet!

Now, back to the other side.

Well, Monday came, and the package went, and Ellie went too, back to the temple grounds. She wanted to pray again, this time to thank Heavenly Father for the miraculous blessing with which He had endowed her. She also wanted to ask Him why she had not gained her testimony earlier, before she was baptized. So, up to the temple grounds, she went.

It was still cold but not snowing, and the sun was shining, so Ellie went back to the front of the temple, sat down on one of the benches, and talked to Heavenly Father. In fact, so many thoughts were going through her mind that she talked and talked and tal... okay, I know you know what I mean. But then, again, Ellie's prayers never were short, so it was no surprise that she was there—on the temple grounds—for quite some time. One of the things she was most interested in learning was why it had taken so long for her to gain her testimony. So that was what she prayed about the most.

As she prayed, she thought about many other times throughout her life when she had questions that no one could answer, so she took them to Heavenly Father. And then, especially when she was young, the answers came quickly. As a matter of fact, there were times when the answers came before she was even done asking the question.

'How did that happen?' You are probably asking.

Well, I will tell you; this is how that happened.

One day, when Ellie was in third grade, and her class was having a science lesson, Mrs. L'Nels, her teacher, had told them that there were reports about the planets lining up in such a way that they were going to cause the 'End of the World.' She explained what that meant by blowing up a balloon to represent the Earth, and then blowing up more balloons to represent each of the other planets. She then lined them up in a row and told the class that, because of the powerful pull of the gravitational fields of all the other planets, the Earth would experience great turmoil.

"There will be earthquakes," she said, "and storms, and tidal waves, and all kinds of massive, uncontrollable natural disasters until..." she stopped briefly to pull a pin out of her desk drawer, then continued, "the Earth explodes." At just that moment, she poked the balloon with the pin and popped it. That, of course, startled the whole class. Every kid, and I do mean EVERY kid, jumped with such vigor that most of them fell off of their chairs. Now, that got almost all of them laughing, but Ellie was not one of those. She was very bothered by what Mrs. L'Nels had said. In fact, that was all she could think about for the rest of the school day.

When school was dismissed, Ellie bounded out of the classroom, scampered through the halls, scooted her way around, what to her, at that moment, seemed like a zabillion kids, and hustled out the door. She ran the three blocks home with all the speed she could muster, broke through the door, not literally, and ran to the dining room where she saw Mommy sitting at the table playing Solitaire. Mommy could see that she was upset about something and was going to ask her what was wrong, but before Mommy could say anything, Ellie reported to her, with all the details, what Mrs. L'Nels had told them.

To Ellie's surprise, Mommy did not seem to be alarmed at all. But she did get up from her chair, walk over to Ellie, gave her a great big 'little hug,' and said, "Ellie, that is not going to happen. I do not know why your teacher told you something so silly. You do not need to worry. Everything will be okay."

After a few more hugs and reassurances, Mommy went back to her cards, and Ellie, still feeling a little unsettled, went out the back door—not to Catalpa—through the yard, out the gate, and to the corner of the garage door frame, where she sat down, put her head in her hands, and began to cry. But within just a few moments, things changed.

Even though Ellie was not looking up, even though her eyes were closed and her hands were covering her face, she could see that there was a light shining. When she looked up to see from where it was coming, she saw a man, dressed in a white robe. In fact, everything about him, his face, his hands, his feet, his hair, everything was brighter than the noon-day sun!

His expression was pleasant, and his voice was soft and gentle when he said, "Ellie, Father has sent me to comfort you. He wants you to know that the world is not going to end. You need not fear. Everything will be okay."

As he spoke, all the bad feelings and woes that Ellie had felt disappeared. Then, as she watched him ascend above the clouds, she felt a wonderful peace that she had never felt before and she knew that everything was going to be okay, and it did.

Now, while I could go on and on, I will not; I will just take you back to the temple grounds, where Ellie is.

Ellie had been sitting and silently praying for a little bit of a while, asking Heavenly Father all of the questions she had in her mind. Why some prayers are answered so quickly and others seem to take longer to be answered than it took for Jesus and the Great and Noble to create the Earth? Well, okay, so that is a bit of an exaggeration, but you know what she meant.

She was also wondering why some prayers were answered in the ways that she wanted them to be answered and other prayers were answered in different ways. Then too, she also wanted to know why some prayers do not seem to be answered at all. But that time, as she sat there, her prayers were answered, and this is what Heavenly Father explained to her.

Not all of the things we want and think we need, are really what is best for us to have. And, even though it may seem to us that when we are praying for something, that is the right time for us to receive it, it may not be the right time. So, we must be careful to not let ourselves believe that we 'know better than He does.'

When we rely upon Him and His wisdom, we will be blessed greatly with what is best for us to have in the time that is best for us to have it. That is how the answers and blessings that we do receive will be able to be of the greatest help to our learning, growth, and development of knowledge, abilities, and progression.

And sometimes, in ways that we may not even be aware of, the right answers and blessings given at the right times, go a long way to enable, not only our advancement, but our protection as well. And more often than we may ever know, the answers and blessings that come from our prayers also help others. So, sometimes, because Heavenly Father knows that we will be okay, even if we have to wait, He will provide those responses at the time that is best, not just for us, but also for those others whom they will help.

And all of that is okay. After all, is that not the best way for us to progress, to align ourselves with Heavenly Father and His one true gospel. His plan for our salvation and eternal progression. That is how we have the opportunity to not just grow and progress, but to do so in the ways that we need to do in order to return to our Heavenly Parents and be a part of Their, Our Eternal Family: *Together Forever!*

Feeling very uplifted and full of joy, Ellie got up from the bench and walked along the path from the front of the Provo Temple to the back of the Provo Temple, then down that same path to the temple grounds entrance, through the gate onto Temple Hill Drive, which took her to Temple View Drive, then back to 900 East, where she continued to Heritage Hall, she said to herself, "Well, **now I know**, not just why Heavenly Father answers our prayers the way

He does, but also how much. Well at least as much as
my mortal brain can comprehend, how much He loves
us!

ABOUT THE AUTHOR

Eileen DiStasio-Clark is the second oldest of four children. She is the mother of eleven children and grandmother to twenty-three grandchildren, to date. As a member of The Church of Jesus Christ of Latter-Day Saints, she serves in various positions, teaching, leading, and ministering to children, youth, and adults. Currently, she is also a Family History Missionary. Eileen established the Pursuit of Excellence Institute of Family Education, a non-profit organization focused on strengthening the family. Presently she holds an A.A., a B.A., and an M.A. in Clinical Psychology and is working on the completion of her Doctoral Degree.